This Little Tiger book belongs to:

_____

_____

_____

For every child who has yet to read Alice's Adventures in Wonderland – you're in for a treat! ~ P B

For Gus, for many wonderful reasons ~ L B

You're invited...

LITTLE TIGER PRESS LTD, an imprint of the Little Tiger Group
1 Coda Studios, 189 Munster Road, London SW6 6AW
www.littletiger.co.uk

First published in Great Britain 2018
This edition published 2019

Text by Poppy Bishop
Text copyright © Little Tiger Press Ltd 2018
Illustrations copyright © Laura Brenlla 2018

Laura Brenlla has asserted her right to be identified as the author and
illustrator of this work under the Copyright, Designs and Patents Act, 1988
A CIP catalogue record for this book is available from the British Library

Printed in China • LTP/1800/2634/0519

10 9 8 7 6 5 4 3 2 1

ALICE'S
Wonderland
TEA PARTY

Poppy Bishop   Laura Brenlla

LITTLE TIGER
LONDON

Alice was having a tea party.
She had sent out perfect, neat invitations
and laid out delicate teacups.
"There," she said to Mad Hatter, "doesn't
that look just right?"

MORE TEA! MORE TEA!

I WONDER WHAT EVERYONE WILL BRING ...

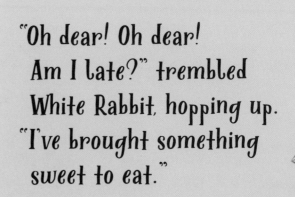

"Oh dear! Oh dear! Am I late?" trembled White Rabbit, hopping up. "I've brought something sweet to eat."

"Clocks?" asked Alice. "Surely we can't eat those?"

"Of course we can!" scoffed Mad Hatter.
"They taste delicious sprinkled with sugar . . .

"Stop being silly!" cried Alice. "This is a proper tea party. I do hope someone brings something ORDINARY to eat."

Not a moment too soon, Dodo arrived.

"Salutations," he said. "I have brought a cake."

"Is it meant to be upside-down?" asked Alice, curiously. "How do we eat it?"

"A topsy-turvy tea party is far too silly," cried Alice. "Everybody turn the right way round this instant!"

The right way up, they heard a rustling in the tree. It was Cheshire Cat with a pie. The pie certainly looked ordinary.

"Does it turn us upside-down?" asked Alice.

"Don't be ridiculous," said Cheshire Cat.

"My pie . . .

Just then a royal trumpet tooted and the Knave of Hearts strode in.

"Tarts for milady's tea party," he bowed.

"At last!" cheered Alice. "Something perfectly ordinary to eat."

QUICK!

HIDE!

"Oh NO," gulped the Mad Hatter, turning pale. "Don't eat THOSE! They belong to . . .

# of HEARTS!

"Those are MINE!" she bellowed.
"Off with their heads!"
And she snatched the tarts
(and the Knave of Hearts) and
took them clean away.

ZZZZZZ

Everybody was starting to feel very hungry, when at last Cook and Duchess arrived.

"Hurrah! Eclairs!" cheered Alice.

"These eclairs," barked the Duchess, "are made with Cook's secret ingredient . . .

zzzzzzz

"Oh dear," sighed Alice. "This is the silliest tea party ever."

Then she looked at her friends and started to giggle. The tea party hadn't been polite or perfectly proper, but it had been FUN.

THERE'S CAKE ON MY HAT!

1/16

"YOU started without ME!"
huffed Caterpillar, wriggling up.
"I'VE brought cupcakes."
"Do they make us sneeze or
disappear?" asked Alice.
"No," said Caterpillar.
"Oh," said Alice, a little
disappointed.

. . . but not for long!
"Did I mention," said Caterpillar, "that my cupcakes are MAGIC!"
"Hurrah!" cheered Alice. "This really is the BEST TEA PARTY EVER!"

THOSE
CUPCAKES MADE
MY EARS GROW!

"Well," sighed Alice, "at last we have something normal to eat."
So they tidied the table and all sat down for a perfectly proper, TERRIBLY ordinary tea party . . .

MY STOMACH FEELS PECULIAR...

More wonderful interactive books from Little Tiger Press

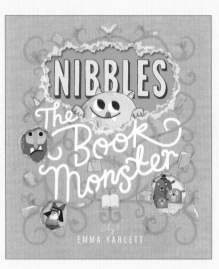

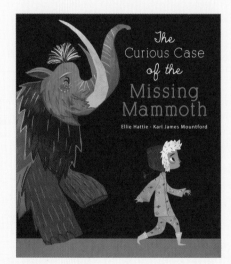

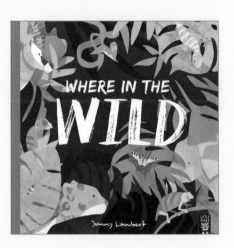

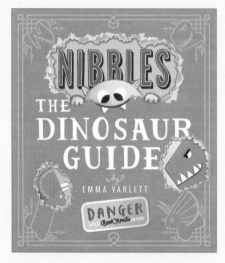

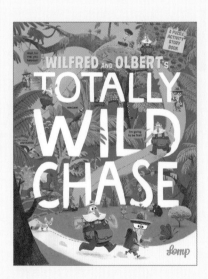

For information regarding any of the above titles or for our catalogue, please contact us:

Little Tiger Press Ltd, 1 Coda Studios, 189 Munster Road, London SW6 6AW

Tel: 020 7385 6333 • E-mail: contact@littletiger.co.uk • www.littletiger.co.uk